USBORNE FIRST READING

Level Four

The Magic Wishbone

Based on a fairy tale by
Charles Dickens

Retold by Mary Sebag-Montefiore

Illustrated by Qin Leng

Reading consultant: Alison Kelly
University of Roehampton

Once upon a time,
a king and queen had...

...nineteen children!

Princess Alice was the eldest.
She took care of them all.

They were very poor, even though they were royal.

On Alice's birthday, the king went to buy a chicken for supper.

As he left the shop, an old woman appeared.

The king jumped in surprise. “Who are you?”

The woman waved her fan. “I’m Alice’s fairy godmother,” she said.

"Oh?" said the king. "I didn't know Alice had one."

"I have a birthday surprise for her," the fairy went on.

"At supper, she will find a wishbone on her plate. Tell her to wash it, dry it and polish it until it shines."

The king frowned. "Her surprise is a *wishbone*?"

"This one is special," said the fairy. "It's magic. But Princess Alice can only use it once."

"It will give her anything... if she wishes at the *right time*."

After supper, Alice did find a wishbone on her plate. So the king told her about her fairy godmother.

The next day, the queen woke up with a terrible headache. "Oh dear!" she gasped, and fainted.

Alice almost took out her magic wishbone...

Instead, she went to look for some medicine.

Then she tidied the palace...

...and made some soup.

After that, she looked after her little brothers and sisters.

She played with them, fed them and cuddled the baby.

The king watched her. "Why doesn't she use the wishbone?" he thought.

"Alice," he said, "where's the magic wishbone?"

"In my pocket, Papa."

"I thought you'd lost it?"

"Oh no, Papa."

"Or forgotten it?"

"No indeed, Papa."

That afternoon, a dog scared Prince Sam. The prince ran away.

He tripped and cut his hand. "Ow!" Sam howled.

His brothers and sisters saw him fall and screamed.

"There, there," said Alice, and she took him to her bedroom.

First, she made a bandage for his hand. Then she made Sam a sling.

"Alice," said the king.
"What are you doing?"

"Snipping and
stitching, Papa."

“Where’s the magic wishbone?”

“In my pocket, Papa.”

“I thought you’d lost it?”

“Oh no, Papa.”

“Or even forgotten it?”

“No indeed, Papa.”

The very next day, the baby princess tumbled over and hurt her lip. She roared.

"There, there," said Alice, picking her up. "I think we all need a treat."

Let's go to
the kitchen and
make cakes.

She made everyone cooks' hats out of paper.

They stirred butter, sugar, eggs and flour, and poured them into tins.

"Delicious!" said Alice, and put them in the oven to bake.

Later, they danced through the palace. Alice saw her father. He was surrounded by bills and looked sad. She stopped.

“What have you been up to, Alice?” asked the king.

“Eating cake, Papa.”

“Where’s the magic wishbone?”

"In my pocket, Papa."

"I thought you'd lost it?"

"Oh no, Papa."

"Or forgotten it?"

"No indeed, Papa."

The king gave a sigh. His lip wobbled and he burst into tears.

Alice was shocked. "What's the matter?" she cried.

"We are so poor I think we will have to sell the palace."

He began to pace around, throwing bills in the air.

"Oh no! Can't you get *any* money?" asked Alice.

"No. I've tried and tried."

At these words, Alice put her hand in her pocket. She felt the magic wishbone.

“I think it is time to wish,”
she said.

She held up the bone, shining like the sun, and made her wish.

At once, golden coins rattled down the chimney and bounced onto the floor.

With a whoosh, Alice's fairy godmother flew into the throne room.

"Do you see why Alice didn't use the wishbone sooner?" she asked the king.

He nodded.

The fairy godmother waved her fan...

...and there was the queen, looking well again.

The palace shimmered and turned gold...

...and the little princes and princesses were dressed in the finest clothes.

The fairy tapped Alice with her fan. Alice's ragged dress became a sparkling gown.

“A beautiful princess needs a prince,” said the fairy. She waved her fan one last time.

A handsome prince appeared.

“My dears,” said the fairy, “let’s have a party.”

"I promise you will all live happily ever after."

"Now," she added, "the wishbone's magic has ended."
She threw it into the fire.

There was a hiss of silver smoke and golden flame. The wishbone vanished forever.

Charles Dickens, who wrote this story, lived in Victorian times. As a boy, his family were so poor, he had to work in a factory. But he grew up to become a rich and famous writer.

Designed by Nelupa Hussain
Series editor: Lesley Sims
Series designer: Russell Punter

First published in 2012 by Usborne Publishing Ltd., Usborne House, 83-85 Saffron Hill, London EC1N 8RT, England. www.usborne.com

UE. First published in America in 2012.

USBORNE FIRST READING
Level Four

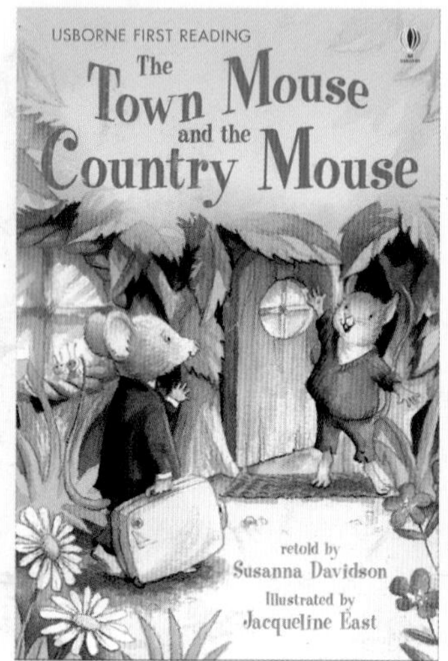

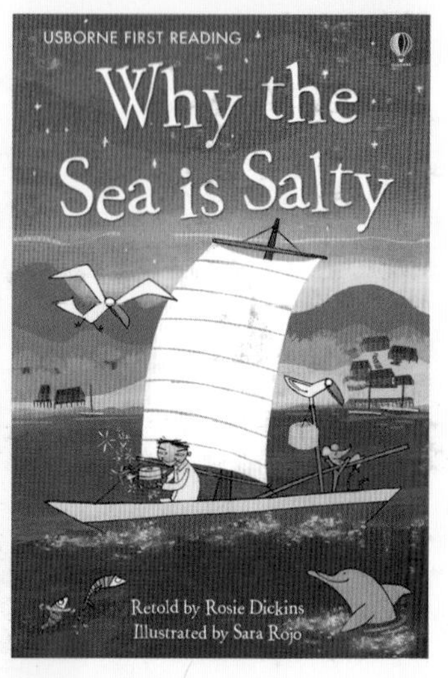